The Dragon and the Unicorn

V O Y A G E R   B O O K S

H A R C O U R T ,   I N C .

San Diego   New York   London

The Dragon and the Unicorn

WRITTEN AND ILLUSTRATED BY LYNNE CHERRY

First Voyager Books edition 1998
Voyager Books is a registered trademark of Harcourt, Inc.

The Library of Congress has cataloged the hardcover edition as follows:
Cherry, Lynne.
The dragon and the unicorn/by Lynne Cherry.
p.   cm.—(A Gulliver Green Book.)
Summary: Valerio the dragon and Allegra the unicorn are driven into hiding
when humans begin to destroy their natural habitat, but they receive hope
when they befriend the daughter of the man responsible.
[1. Dragons—Fiction. 2. Unicorns—Fiction. 3. Conservation of natural
resources—Fiction.] I. Title. II. Series.
PZ7.C4199Dr   1995
[Fic]—dc20   92-30321
ISBN 0-15-224193-0
ISBN 0-15-201888-3 pb

K J I H

Printed in Singapore

The paintings in this book were done in Pentel watercolors on
Strathmore 400 watercolor paper.
The display type was set in Duc De Berry.
The text type was set in Van Dijck.
Color separations by Bright Arts, Ltd., Singapore
Printed and bound by Tien Wah Press, Singapore
Production supervision by Stanley Redfern and Jane Van Gelder
Designed by Michael Farmer and Linda Lockowitz

ACKNOWLEDGMENTS

For the use of their photographs as reference, thank you to:
photographer Gary Braasch, who allowed me to work from the
beautiful photographs in his book *Secrets of the Old Growth Forest*,
written by David Kelly, published by Gibbs Smith Publisher,
P.O. Box 667, 1877 East Gentile Street, Layton, Utah 84041; and
photographer Trygve Steen, who sent me his own photographs
to work from and nature guides of the Cascades and Pacific
Northwest forest.

For providing me with reference material, thank you to: Willamette
National Forest, which lent me slides; Stephen Whitney, author of
the Audubon Society's nature guide *Western Forests*; Daniel Mathews,
author of *Cascade-Olympic Natural History*, published by Raven Editions
in conjunction with the Portland Audubon Society; Senator Gaylord
Nelson, Steve Whitney, and Maureen Maxwell of the Wilderness
Society; The Olympic National Park; Glacier National Park; and The
Nature Conservancy.

Thank you to those who posed for the characters in the book: the
lovely Lena Jackson of Washington, D.C., who posed for the princess;
the handsome Patrick Ukata, who posed for the king; the gorgeous
Bahim Hisan of Ba-HI Black Arabians in Charlotte Hall, Maryland,
who posed for Allegra the Unicorn; and Bahim Hisan's owners, Susan
Riley Canterbury and James W. Canterbury.

Thank you to Scott McVay and Alexandra Christie for their support
of environmental literature for children.

Thank you to Coy Batson for helping me name Allegra while riding
down a Texas highway.

Thanks to Liz Van Doren for her patience and Rubin Pfeffer for
his solace.

Thank you to my friend Tim Hermach, Native Forest Council,
Eugene, Oregon, for reading the manuscript for accuracy.

Thank you to: the Native Forest Council, Eugene, Oregon; the
Wilderness Society, Washington, D.C.; the Rainforest Action Group,
San Francisco, California; Earthroots Coalition, Toronto, Canada; and
the many other groups and individuals fighting to save the national
treasure of our native and old growth forests.

*For information on how you can help preserve and protect old
growth forests write to the Center for Children's Environmental
Literature, P.O. Box 5995, Washington, D.C. 20016-5995.*

To the over one hundred authors and illustrators of
the Center for Children's Environmental Literature
and
to Dad, who taught me to love the forest, and
to Mom, who encouraged me to paint it

THERE WAS a dragon named Valerio, who lived on a lovely
mountaintop overlooking a long, winding river, a blue lake,
and the ancient tall trees of the Ardet Forest. Each morning
upon waking, Valerio would lumber down to the lake. Lifting his

wings to catch the wind, he would sail to the end of the lake to the giant redwood forest—the home of Allegra the unicorn. Allegra was as old as the Ardet Forest. She was the wisest and gentlest of all the forest creatures.

Together, the dragon and the unicorn would run through the forest, past the Ardet Waterfall, and along the Ardet River as it splashed and gurgled its way to the sea.

They found delicious treats during their journeys through the forest. At the edge of the woods grew blackberry bushes. On the hill they ate blueberries, strawberries, huckleberries, and raspberries. Around the marshes they savored wild asparagus and the roots of Queen Anne's lace.

Valerio and Allegra lived in harmony with the land and all the other creatures of the fields, forests, and streams—wolves, foxes, finches, deer, fish, raccoons, and rabbits.

One morning when Valerio opened his large eyes and looked out upon his beautiful view, he saw something new and strange. Smoke. He went to investigate, thinking, *Perhaps it is another dragon.*

There, in a clearing in the woods, was a creature Valerio had never seen before, surrounded by many fallen trees. The creature walked upright on two legs instead of four. It had neither fur nor feathers nor scales. It had created a fire—like the fire Valerio sometimes breathed from his mouth when he was very scared.

Valerio ran to find Allegra, and for several days they watched as this creature and others like him cut down trees, made a shelter, cut down more and more trees, built more fires, and began to make more shelters all along the hillside.

Valerio was worried. And so was Allegra. *She* knew who these creatures were. "They are humans," she told Valerio. "Beware of them."

Instead of running through the forest, Valerio and Allegra now spent their days watching the leader, whose name was King Orlando, as he worked. After the trees fell, they noticed, his child ran to pick up the birds' nests. She carefully cupped them in her hands and placed them in the branches of safer trees deeper in the woods.

Soon the humans began to build a huge fortress. As spring turned into summer, the castle walls grew and so did the trouble. The king had heard that the horn of the unicorn contained magic powers. He sent his knights, fierce-looking humans on horseback, through the woods to search for her. Allegra hid deeper and deeper in the forest. When winter snow fell and their whole world was white, she was camouflaged and could not be found. But as the next spring turned the ground green and brown, Allegra was much too easy to see. So she rolled in the mud to color herself brown and ran with the deer.

One day the humans found Allegra washed clean after a long, hard rain. The pileated woodpecker saw her fighting against the king's knights and flew as fast as her wings would carry her to Valerio's cave.

Valerio thundered through the forest. He came upon the knights throwing ropes around Allegra's neck. Coated in armor and carrying sharp weapons, the knights were frightening.

During the awful battle, Valerio was so frightened that he breathed more smoke and fire than he ever had before. The huge billows of smoke caused the knights' eyes to burn and sting. While they coughed and gasped for air, Valerio burned the ropes and Allegra broke free.

The next day King Orlando pronounced to all his knights that he who slayed the dragon would receive riches enough to befit a prince. Now neither Allegra nor Valerio was safe.

Allegra had gone into hiding in a cave behind the Ardet Waterfall, where her form dissolved into the white mist. Valerio joined her there. And so it was that both the dragon and the unicorn came to live in hiding. During their days in the cave behind the waterfall, Valerio and Allegra tried to figure out how to save themselves *and* the Ardet Forest.

The other animals of the forest missed the dragon and the unicorn and mourned the destruction of their homes. One day a small, brave sparrow flew to King Orlando's fortress and over the castle walls.

"I have discovered that the humans are *afraid* of the forest and of the creatures that live in it!" she told her friends when she returned. "They think it is dark and dangerous and that we will harm them! They think the forest magic lies within the unicorn's horn. This is why they want to capture you, Allegra! But one young girl, the daughter of the king, is not afraid. She smells the flowers, watches the birds, and sometimes sits so calm and still that we are not afraid to approach her. Her name is Arianna."

"She may be able to help us!" said Allegra. "We must lure her into the depths of our forest and let it work its magic upon her!"

The next day, as Arianna wandered near the forest, Allegra emerged from the trees and stood before her. Arianna stared as the unicorn pawed the ground and shook her mane. The princess followed Allegra deep into the forest until they came to the Ardet Waterfall.

But as Valerio emerged from behind the waterfall, the princess became frightened. Her father had told her that dragons were evil and terrifying. Before she could run away, the unicorn went up to Valerio and rubbed her nose against his. Arianna watched but stayed where she was.

The forest was always dark, but with evening approaching it grew darker. The spring peepers began their nocturnal symphony. Owls hooted, bullfrogs croaked, and a marbled murrelet called. Arianna was afraid, but the unicorn drew close and comforted her, and the dragon draped his wings protectively around them both. They all fell to sleep to the music of the night.

The princess awoke, smiling, to the morning songs of cedar waxwings. The dragon and the unicorn led her to the places where the wild berries grew. She tasted the wild asparagus and wild carrot root. They all drank together from a clean, sparkling stream. Thus they spent their days and by the end of the first week, the king's daughter had lost her desire to return to the castle.

One day Arianna asked the unicorn, "How old are you, Allegra?"

"I'm as old as the forest," Allegra answered.

"How old is the forest?" asked Arianna.

"Older than its trees. Let me show you how old its trees are."

Valerio lifted Arianna onto Allegra's back, and they fairly flew through the forest to the place King Orlando had cleared. Allegra stopped at an enormous fallen tree.

"Each year, as a tree grows, a ring of new growth is formed. When the tree is cut or falls, we can see those rings and count the age of the tree," she said.

Arianna leaned over and began to count the tree rings. After a long time she gasped. "Six hundred tree rings!"

"This tree is six hundred years old," said Allegra. "But the forest was a forest before this tree was a seedling. The forest is many thousands of years old. Humans think I only have magic, but most of my power comes from knowledge. And this forest contains more wisdom than I could ever have. Tell your father to explore it and learn about the millions of things living in this forest. It will teach you things about yourselves and about the world in which you live."

Allegra pointed to a yew tree and continued, "Many, many years from now a disease will come to humans that only the bark of this tree can cure. But what if you have cut down all the yew trees? And your people will be visited by other illnesses. The cures may be in this golden mushroom or this flower or this vine or this moss hanging from the branches above us. You must not destroy the forest. Your life is tied to the life of the forest." Allegra's words surprised Arianna. She had never thought about all the years past and all the years to come.

Valerio and Allegra also showed Arianna how her father had harmed their world—the altered view from the mountaintop, felled trees, and crushed eggshells. "As my father's castle grows, your forest is shrinking. At this pace it will all be gone someday," Arianna said to her new friends. The dragon and the unicorn looked at her sadly.

"I'm sorry my father is making your lives so miserable," Arianna continued. "He's not a bad man. He just doesn't understand." She hesitated. "In fact, he must be sick with worry about me."

Arianna was right. When the king had discovered his daughter's disappearance, he sent out all his knights to find her. But just as they had failed to find the dragon or unicorn in their hiding place, they could not find the king's daughter.

The king could not be consoled. Arianna's mother, Queen Helen, said to him, "Orlando, perhaps you should go quietly into the forest and try to find Arianna yourself." But the king did not heed his wife's words. He continued to send out his knights while he remained in the castle with a heavy heart, afraid to go into the forest himself.

Then one day, after weeks had passed, King Orlando rode his horse to the edge of the woods, dismounted, and walked into the forest. The sounds were unfamiliar and strange.

The king walked farther and, shivering from fright, sat down at the foot of an enormous tree. He pulled his cape around himself, remembering myths about people becoming bewitched or being transformed into trees forever! But he thought of his daughter and kept going.

For several days King Orlando wandered through the forest. When he was hungry, he ate wild berries. When he was thirsty, he drank from the streams. All the time, he felt as if he was being watched, and indeed he was. The animals of the forest were aware of his presence, and the unicorn, with her magic, was drawing him toward the Ardet Waterfall.

The next day King Orlando reached the waterfall. He rested on a rock with the tumbling water at his back. The singing of the birds echoed throughout the forest. *What beautiful sounds*, he thought. The trunks of the ancient trees rose straight and tall from the forest floor, arching far above like flying buttresses. "Why, this forest is like a cathedral!" he said aloud. The thundering waterfall sprayed its mist around him. "A rainbow!" he exclaimed. "Oh, how Arianna loved rainbows! I would do anything to have her with me now."

Then, in a moment, she was. "Oh, Father, Father!" she shouted as she threw herself into his arms.

But to the king's surprise, Arianna did not want to go back to the castle immediately. Instead she showed her father her favorite places and also the places where the forest had been destroyed. King Orlando exclaimed, "I never realized what peace, silence, and beauty lay within the darkness of the forest. I had no idea that it was so full of *life*—and so many *different kinds* of living things!"

"Father," Arianna said, "you wanted to capture the unicorn and kill her to get her magic. But the unicorn's magic is *knowledge*. In order to teach us, Allegra must remain alive and free. And the dragon, Valerio, is kind and gentle. He is Allegra's friend and protector."

When she trusted that her father understood, Arianna took him to meet the dragon and the unicorn. To them the king said, "My knights will hunt you no longer. Instead they will explore the forest's mysteries and hunt for its secrets."

When they had said their farewells and promised to come back and visit, Arianna and her father returned to the castle. King Orlando proclaimed that the remaining forest would be preserved as it was that very day. No more trees would be cut, no more earth dug in this ancient forest. To his people he said, "We will learn to love and respect this forest, and it will tell us its secrets."

As years passed, houses were built and the village became a town. But King Orlando's decree lived on for centuries— and up until the present time. The Ardet Forest remains a haven for all living things. For people, it is a place to find peace and silence. But for animals, and for the dragon and the unicorn, it is home.